For Lily and Petunia, with love! —L.N.
For Donna and Phil Hinko —F.B.

If You Give a Cat a Cupcake

If You Give a

Cat a Cupcake

WRITTEN BY Laura Numeroff

ILLUSTRATED BY Felicia Bond

Laura Geringer Books
An Imprint of HarperCollins*Publishers*

If You Give a Cat a Cupcake
Text copyright © 2008 by Laura Numeroff
Illustrations copyright © 2008 by Felicia Bond

Library of Congress Cataloging-in-Publication Data
Numeroff, Laura Joffe.
  If you give a cat a cupcake / by Laura Numeroff ; illustrated by Felicia Bond.
— 1st ed.
    p.   cm.
  Summary: A series of increasingly far-fetched events might occur if someone were
to give a cupcake to a cat.
  ISBN 978-0-06-028324-7 (trade bdg.) — ISBN 978-0-06-028325-4 (lib bdg.)
  [1. Cats—Fiction.] I. Bond, Felicia, ill. II. Title.
PZ7.N9641c 2008   2008005860
[E]—dc22   CIP
                                                                      AC

1 2 3 4 5 6 7 8 9 10   ❖   First Edition

 is a registered trademark of
HarperCollins Publishers

If you give a cat a cupcake,

he'll ask for some sprinkles to go with it.

When you give him the sprinkles,
he might spill some on the floor.

Cleaning up will make him hot,
so you'll give him a bathing suit

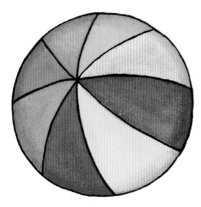

and take him to the beach.

He'll want to go in the water

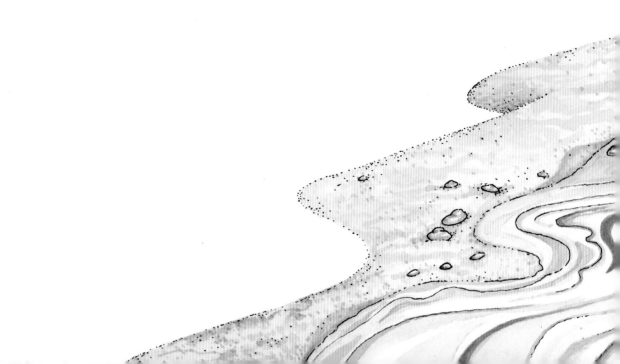

and build a sand castle, too.

Then he'll look for seashells.

He'll find a few other things as well.

He'll put them in his pail and try to pick it up,
but it'll be too heavy.

He'll decide he needs to work out at the gym.

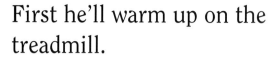
First he'll warm up on the treadmill.

Then he'll lift a weight or two.

He might even try a karate class.

After the gym, he'll want to go to the park.
When you get there, he'll see the rocks.
He'll climb as high as he can go.

At the top, he'll see the lake.
He'll want you to take him rowing.

He'll be the captain,
and you'll have to row.

Then he'll notice the merry-go-round and want to go for a ride.

He'll want you to go for a ride, too.

You'll choose the horse with the purple mane,
and he'll get on the whale.

The whale will remind him
of the science museum.
He'll ask you to take him there.

First he'll find the

dinosaurs.

Then he'll visit the

Hall of Apes.

When the museum closes,
you'll be the last to leave.

On the way home, you'll pass by the beach.
You'll help him gather all of his things.

Then he'll want to race you.

When you get home, he'll empty
the sand from his shoes.
He might spill some on the floor.

Seeing the sand on the floor
will remind him of the sprinkles.

He'll probably ask you for some.

And chances are,

if you give him some sprinkles,

he'll want a cupcake to go with them.